LEVEL
1
Reader

DREAM
GABBY'S
DOLLHOUSE

PANDY'S BAD DAY

Adapted by **GABRIELLE REYES**

SCHOLASTIC INC.

Pandy Paws is having a bad day.

First, he fell in the kitchen.

Then he found a hole in his bag.

Next, his tail got stuck in
Cat-A-Vator's doors.

Nothing is going right today!

"I'm sorry about your bad day,"
says Gabby. "Everyone has a bad
day sometimes. Even me!"

"What helps when you're having a bad day?" Pandy Paws asks.

"I ask my friends for help!"

"Maybe the Gabby Cats can help!"
Gabby says.

Pandy Paws says, "Let's give it
a go!"

They go to the craft room to visit
Baby Box.

Gabby asks, "What helps you on a bad day?"

"I make things, like kitty faces with rocks."

Pandy Paws picks a rock.

He feels sad, so he makes it into a sad kitty.

9

Gabby adds a face to her rock, too!

Then Baby Box has a surprise.

"I fixed your bag!"

Pandy Paws feels better.

Then his paw gets all sticky!

Gabby and Pandy Paws visit Carlita next.

"What helps you on bad days?" Gabby asks.

"I move my body!"

Pandy Paws hops on Carlita's bounce pad.

He bounces . . .

and bounces . . .

and bounces!

Pandy Paws feels better.

Then he bounces too high!

Gabby helps him get down.

In the garden, Pandy Paws asks Kitty Fairy, "What helps you on bad days?

"I sit outside and just breathe, like this . . ."

Close your
eyes.

Breathe in slowly
and fill your belly.

Then breathe
out.

Pandy Paws closes his eyes.

He breathes in and fills his belly.

Then he breathes out.

He opens his eyes and smiles.

"Hi, butterfly!" he says.

Pandy Paws feels better.

Then it starts to rain!

The friends visit DJ Catnip inside.

Pandy Paws asks, "What helps you on bad days?"

"I bang on the drums and sing it out!" says DJ Catnip.

Pandy Paws gives it a go.

Bang!

Bang, bang!

Bang, bang, bang!

He feels a lot better.

Then his drum breaks!

CatRat arrives!

"Sometimes I like bad days. They make good days feel even better," says CatRat.

Surprise!

DJ Catnip fixed Pandy Paws' drum.

"Good as new!"

Kitty Fairy, Baby Box, and Carlita
visit the music room to check
on Pandy Paws.

Pandy Paws tells them about his day.

"My bad day had some good parts, too!"

Pandy Paws loves spending time with his best friends, especially on bad days!

"I have the best friends in the world!"
Pandy Paws says.

Now that Pandy Paws feels better,
he has a question for you.

"What makes you feel better when you have a bad day?"